Kids love reading
Choose Your Own Adventure®!

D0189441

FORECAST FROM STONEHENGE

BY R. A. MONTGOMERY

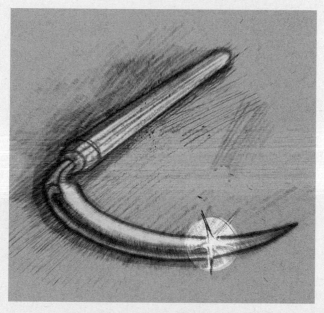

ILLUSTRATED BY VLADIMIR SEMIONOV
COVER ILLUSTRATED BY WES LOUIE

CHOOSECO®
WAITSFIELD, VERMONT

Book design: Stacey Boyd, Big Eyedea Visual Design

For information regarding permission, write to:

CHOOSECO

P.O. Box 46, Waitsfield, Vermont 05673
www.cyoa.com

Publisher's Cataloging-In-Publication Data

Names: Montgomery, R. A. | Semionov, Vladimir,
illustrator. | Louie, Wes, illustrator.
Title: Forecast from Stonehenge / by R.A. Montgomery ;
illustrated by Vladimir Semionov ; cover illustrated by
Wes Louie.
Other Titles: Choose your own adventure ; 19.
Description: Waitsfield, Vermont : Chooseco, [2006] |
Summary: You're traveling to Salisbury, England, to
research the megalithic arrangement at Stonehenge, as
well as some unusual crop circles nearby. Time is of the
essence--world leaders gather in worry as hurricanes
rip cross-continent, tropical storms surge inland,
and animals' strange new migration patterns cause
environmentalists extreme concern. What will you do?
Identifiers: ISBN 1-933390-19-0 | ISBN 978-1-933390-19-2
Subjects: LCSH: Stonehenge (England)--Juvenile fiction.
| Crop circles--England--Juvenile fiction. | Global
environmental change--Juvenile fiction. | CYAC: Stonehenge
(England)--Fiction. | Crop circles--England--Fiction. |
Global environmental change--Fiction. | LCGFT: Detective
and mystery fiction. | Choose-your-own stories.
Classification: LCC PZ7.M7684 Fo 2006 | DDC [Fic]--dc23

To Ramsey and Anson
And to Avery and Lila

And to Shannon

BEWARE and WARNING!

This book is different from other books.

You and YOU ALONE are in charge of what happens in this story.

There are dangers, choices, adventures, and consequences. YOU must use all of your numerous talents and much of your enormous intelligence. The wrong decision could end in disaster—even death. But don't despair. At any time, YOU can go back and make another choice, alter the path of your story, and change its result.

You travel to Stonehenge on the summer solstice, the most sacred day in the Druid calendar. You are supposed to meet a man named Alastair who knows something about the famously missing heelstone of Stonehenge. But when you arrive, the site is crowded with all sorts of people dressed in costume for the special day. You must exercise caution as not everyone is who they appear to be. If you find Alastair, he could lead you to archaeological fame and fortune—or to certain death. Are you ready to learn the ancient, dark secrets that Stonehenge has in store for you?

You have been back home in London, England for less than two hours when your cell phone rings. You check the incoming number.

"Hello, Twig," you say before your best friend can say anything.

"Ha! You're back. I need your help to do something," your friend replies.

"Hey, Twig, how about a 'nice to have you home' or 'how was Greece?' I've been away three weeks," you say.

"No time for chit chat," Twig snaps. "This is serious. Besides, I know you had a good time in Greece because I read your blog."

"Okay, what's the problem then?" you ask.

"I need you to go to Stonehenge. Today. To meet someone," Twig replies.

Turn to the next page.

2

"Why don't you go? You mean *the* Stonehenge?" In your mind you see the ancient stone monument that sits on the Salisbury Plain. For 5,000 years people have wondered how the huge stones were put so precisely in place. And what they were used for.

"I can't go," Twig croaks. "Six broken ribs and a cracked collarbone."

Before you can ask how he broke all those bones, Twig reads your thoughts. "Over the weekend," he says. "Rock climbing in Sussex. I fell. Can't leave bed for two weeks. But if you will go to this meeting for me, I will be on standby."

"Standby for what?" you ask incredulously.

"In case you get in trouble," Twig replies.

Then it occurs to you. Today is June 21st, the summer solstice. It's the longest day of the year. It's also the day the sun will set exactly between the two largest stones, or megaliths, at the site. The Druids who worshiped at Stonehenge considered it the most sacred day of the year. Or at least that is what people now think.

"But I didn't think people were allowed near Stonehenge on the solstice," you say.

"Not for the past thirty years," Twig replies. "But the authorities have decided to open it this year, with heavy police escort."

"Who am I supposed to meet?" you ask. "And why?"

Go on to the next page.

"A fellow named Alastair Shepherd. He claims he has information on the missing heelstone."

"Really?" you say. "The heelstone?" Finally, you are intrigued.

The missing heelstone is a Stonehenge controversy. It stems back to the very first known photograph of Stonehenge taken in 1853. Many of the stones had fallen over. Then in the 1920s, the henge was rebuilt. And one of the stones from the 1853 photo disappeared: the heelstone.

"How do you know that this Alastair is not just some kook?" you ask.

"Well, I don't. But it's worth a meeting. Listen, there's not much time. I suggest a cab."

You glance at your watch. 6:00 PM. About three hours till sundown.

"Okay, I'll go."

"I knew you would do it," Twig says. "I'll cover expenses of course."

"Of course," you reply. "Where am I supposed to meet this Alastair Shepherd again?"

"Just inside the outer ring of megaliths at sunset," Twig replies. "He said he's about five foot six, plump, with a silver beard. He'll be wearing a Druid's cloak with silver embroidery on the sleeves and he'll be carrying a small brown leather satchel."

Turn to the next page.

4

Two hours later your taxi is pulling up to the car park across the road from the Stonehenge monument. Civilian cars were forced to park several miles back in the town of Amesbury. It was sheer luck they were letting taxis in this close. You pay the driver 80 pounds and climb out. It looks like the celebrations have already started. There is a large crowd gathered. Almost everyone is dressed in costume. It takes you a few minutes to realize that no one is moving.

"What's going on?" you ask a young man dressed as Pan, the Greek god of nature.

"They say they aren't going to allow anyone in to the site," he replies, playing a few notes on his pipes. "Something about a terrorist threat against the monument."

"Great," you mutter. It's beginning to look like another of Twig's wild schemes. You call him on your cell phone to ask if there's a Plan B, but the reception is terrible. You get cut off three times before giving up.

You scan the crowd. There are a large number of people dressed as Druids, with gray, hooded robes. But no one has silver thread on their sleeves. Suddenly, a small woman dressed as a fairy, with sparkles on her face and gossamer blue wings, flutters up to you.

"Hi, I'm Elaine," she says in a clear but soft voice.

"Hi," you nod.

"You look like the curious sort," she replies. "Do you want to get in to see the henge?"

Turn to the next page.

6

"Sure, but I am meeting someone first," you say. You notice Elaine is wearing a strange perfume in addition to her fairy outfit. It is very strong, and you are not sure that you really care for it. "I was supposed to meet him inside the outer circle of megaliths at sunset, but I don't see how I can make that appointment."

"I can get you into the henge," she says. "You can come with me and my friends."

You look up and see Elaine's friends all staring at the two of you. They are all dressed as fairies, men and women both. Some have wings, others don't. Everyone seems to sparkle and flash in the waning rays of sunset light.

"There are too many cops to sneak past," you say, pointing to the police spread out in a circle around the monument.

"We know an underground passage. The entrance is just on the other side of this barrow," she says, pointing to the low-lying hill that you are standing on. "Who are you waiting to meet?"

"That's the problem. I've never met him before. He's going to be dressed as a Druid but in this crowd that's not much help."

"We took some Druids through the passage, earlier. Maybe he is already inside?"

"Really? Did one of them have silver thread on his sleeves?"

"Alastair?" She gasps his name. "Why are you meeting Alastair?"

Turn to page 8.

8

"You know him?" you ask, trying to remember if you had mentioned his name before. You don't think so, but your brain seems to be working in slow motion. Maybe you are just tired from all your traveling? Or is it Elaine's odd perfume?

"Of course, I know of him. Alastair is one of the Arch-Druids. Why don't you come with us? Then you won't miss your meeting."

If you choose to stay and keep looking for Alastair outside of the gates, go on to the next page.

If you decide to take Elaine's offer and go into the tunnel in the barrow-mound, turn to page 19.

"Thanks, Elaine, but I'll wait here for Alastair just in case."

A dark scowl comes over her face, but it fades quickly to be replaced by a fake smile. "Your loss. Most would not pass up such an opportunity," she says as she skips over to her friends.

The sun sets as you make your way through the crowded car park. It is late, and a number of people clad in togas sing loudly as the sun dips. Even though you are far from the circle of stones, you feel a jolt of energy. A huge cheer goes up from the crowd, and drums beat. Dancers dressed in kilts with their faces painted blue try to get others to join in the dance.

You keep scanning the crowd but still no Alastair. Peering through the bars of the gates to the henge, you can't see anyone in among the giant stones.

Someone taps you on the shoulder and says, "Sorry about the mix-up on the meeting place. I think you're looking for me. I'm Alastair."

You whirl around.

Turn to page 11.

"Alastair Shepherd?" You are facing a man in a gray Druid's robe. He's not as plump as you expected but otherwise he matches Twig's description. His hood is pulled back, and he smiles at you kindly in the fading light.

"I thought we were going to miss one another." You reach to shake his hand. He clasps onto his walking stick instead, and hands you a package.

"I don't have much time, the others will miss me before too long." His eyes dart around but no one else seems to notice him. He has handed you a small box wrapped in plain brown paper and tied with string. He smiles broadly and does not look at it. "Keep your eyes on me," he urges. "Don't look at the package."

"What's in it?" you ask. Again his eyes dart nervously around.

"It's the ceremonial Golden Sickle passed down by 147 generations of the Suns of Stonehenge." He then says something in a language you don't recognize. "Put it away now! Please," he commands.

"Why don't we get out of this crowd and talk somewhere private," you say, glancing at the boisterous crowd all around you.

"Staying in the crowd is safer. Sometimes they have me watched. We can't talk for long anyway," he says.

You casually stow the package in your pack. "I thought you had information for Twig about the heelstone."

Alastair grabs your hand, clutching it hard. "Forget that!"

Turn to the next page.

"Hey," you say, pulling away. He is no longer smiling, and the increasing darkness makes him seem sinister.

"I need you to take the Golden Sickle to the British Museum. You must see Standish Bloom, the head of the Ceremonial Antiquities Department. He will know its importance."

"Will he meet with me?" you ask.

"Just mention the Golden Sickle from the Suns of Stonehenge, and mention my name," Alastair says. This time he smiles, but it seems forced. You look down at his robe and see that the silver thread makes an intricate pattern along the edges of his sleeves. It looks like writing. "I must go. I am doing a grievous betrayal to the Great Oak even to be telling you of these things. If I am found out, well, you would never see me again."

With that, he turns away from you and disappears into the crowd. Instead of getting smaller, the crowd seems to have grown since the setting of the sun.

Exhausted from the long day and strange events, you catch a ride to Amesbury with a van of elves. You are able to get the last room in a small inn above a pub. When you are safely in your room with the door shut and locked, you extract Alastair's package from your pack.

Go on to the next page.

You carefully untie the string. As soon as you open the paper, you feel your weariness drop away in a surge of adrenaline. The object in your hands is one of the most amazing things you have ever seen. It's a wickedly curved dagger with a sharp interior edge. Fine scrollwork lines both sides of the blade. It contains writing of some sort. A thin runnel curves along the blade's outside edge. And most amazing of all, it does indeed appear to be solid gold! It gleams in the weak lamplight. The handle is made of a smooth, dark wood, and is also intricately carved.

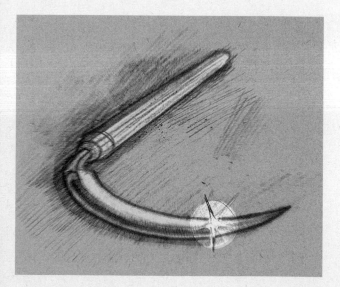

Turn to the next page.

14

Your first impulse is to take a photo of the Golden Sickle with your cell phone camera and send it to Twig. But you don't want to draw attention to yourself by using your flash, and the light in your room is dim. You won't be able to take a decent photo until morning. Besides, Twig is probably already asleep.

If you decide to take a photo of the Golden Sickle anyway, and send it to Twig right away, go on to the next page.

If you decide to wait and take a better photo in the morning, turn to page 16.

You decide to take the photo now so that it's waiting in Twig's inbox when he wakes up. You pull the lampshade off the small lamp next to your bed. You place the sickle on the table as close to the light as possible. You take several snapshots, select the best one and send it to Twig with the following text:

> Interesting developments. See attached. Even more amazing in person. Must bring to British Museum, but want you to take a look first. Call me asap in AM.

You select Twig's name and hit "Send." Then you replace the lampshade and carefully pack up the Golden Sickle and put it away in your pack. As you climb into bed, you think back over the events of your meeting with Alastair. You remember the strange words he spoke when he handed over the sickle. They were from a language you had never heard before. *Twish nathaya nith.* Or something like that. What did they mean, and why did he say them? *I'll have to remember to tell Twig that detail*, you think with a yawn. In seconds you are sound asleep.

Turn to page 29.

16

You decide to wait to take a picture of the sickle in the morning.

You carefully rewrap the ancient object, and place it deep inside your backpack. Minutes later you are changed into pajamas and asleep.

Your dreams are vivid and scary. You are out at Stonehenge alone, and it is night. There is a terrible thunderstorm raging. You walk across the field toward the monument. You can hear sounds of chanting from the innermost circle of stones. You walk carefully and silently forward and turn the corner to see a circle of Druids holding a small wailing lamb to the sky. Is it a sacrifice? You stumble forward on the uneven ground and one of the Druids hears you.

"Intruder!" he yells. Everyone turns at once. One of the Druids begins running toward you. You cannot see his face in the dark hooded robe, but he has a huge gleaming sickle raised to attack.

Aaarrrgghrr!

You bolt upright, awake. It takes you a moment to realize where you are. Is someone outside your door? It sounds like they are trying to pick the lock.

"Who's there?" you yell out in the dark.

Suddenly total silence.

Go on to the next page.

You wait for several minutes. Was it your imagination? All is still. Finally you fall back to sleep. When you open your eyes, your room is flooded with sun, and the clock says 8:15.

I'll get a great picture of the sickle now, you think, hopping off the bed. Once again, when you pull the sickle out of its wrapping, it has that same mesmerizing effect. It almost glows from within. You swing it through the air with a *swiiiishhh*.

Thirty minutes later, you've sent some photos to Twig and had some toast and tea. You check out and head to the train station. While you wait, you call Twig's cell, but it sends you to voicemail.

"Take a look in your inbox, Twig," you say. "I'm on my way back to London now. There's something you need to see."

Alastair told you to go straight to Standish Bloom at the British Museum. But you really want Twig to see the amazing sickle first. When you pull into Waterloo Station, you need to decide. Twig's cell is still sending you to voicemail.

If you decide to go to Twig's house in person before going to the museum, turn to the next page.

If you decide to go to the British Museum right away, turn to page 30.

18

You decide to head to Twig's. He is always on his cell phone. He might not even have received the photo yet. You follow the crowd off the platform and out to the station exit. It's raining and the line for cabs is long. But you have a special technique learned from your Uncle Ben. Two blocks away, there's a cab stand and hardly ever a wait. What's a two block walk compared to a twenty minute wait?

Quite a lot, it turns out.

You have failed to notice the man and woman who have followed you from Amesbury. They are delighted to see you leave the station on foot. Less than a half block from the station they relieve you of your backpack. Just for good measure they bind your hands, feet, and mouth before stowing you in a dumpster behind an office building.

It looks like it's the end of the adventure of the Golden Sickle. You just pray that someone finds you before the weekend…

The End

"You can take me to Alastair?" you ask.

"He and the other Arch-Druids use our entrance," Elaine replies. "Come with me."

She takes you by the hand and introduces you to the others dressed like fairies. Everyone you meet laughs or claps you on the back as if you were old friends. Some even hug you.

"Welcome, human!" one shouts. *These people are pretty good at role-playing*, you think to yourself.

"Hush," hisses Elaine. "Dani, you go distract the guards for a moment. That's all we'll need."

"You got it, boss!" says Dani, giving a sharp salute. You can't tell if she is trying to be funny or not. She bounces away towards the guards. Seconds later she is doing standing flips right in front of them.

Elaine whispers, "Now is our chance."

You step away from the crowd toward the far side of the barrow. When you turn its corner, you are almost out of sight. Elaine wades through the tall grasses. You continue to follow.

Turn to the next page.

20

There is an oval wooden door set into the side of the tall mound. The door has thick wooden pegs and elaborate carvings, but no handle. Elaine quickly taps out a complicated knock on the door.

Go on to the next page.

It whips inward and a small hand reaches out and gestures to you to get inside. You follow Elaine into the dark doorway and down a steep winding hallway lit by torches.

Turn to the next page.

22

Elaine turns one last corner, and you stumble forward into a gigantic dining hall. It might be the largest room you have ever seen. Wooden tables stretch out to the far corners of the room. Hundreds of places are set and most seats are occupied. Everyone is dressed like a fairy, laughing and talking. People throw confetti and there seems to be a flying contest on the far side of the room. You don't see a single person in the gray robes of an Arch-Druid.

"Elaine, I don't see a single Druid," you say. "I thought you said Alastair would be here."

"Well, I thought he could be. I'll ask," she replies cheerfully. She approaches a tall, thin man walking past.

"Alastair?" he answers, stroking his chin. "The Druids departed some time ago for the henge. Thataway," he adds pointing to a large door at the opposite side of the hall. "But I don't think Alastair was with them."

Just then a beautiful woman dressed in green velvet stands on a chair and rings a crystal bell. "Welcome, and let the festivities begin!" A huge cheer goes out, the side doors open, and waiters begin streaming out with platters heaped with food.

"Would you like to eat?" Elaine asks.

The food looks delicious: juicy roasts, steaming mashed potatoes, salads, condiments, pies, and cakes. Your stomach rumbles.

"I'd like to find Alastair," you answer. Someone walks past with a tray of glistening lasagna that smells delicious. It couldn't hurt to take a quick bite.

Turn to page 24.

24

Your mouth is salivating. Then you remember something from pre-school. It was a line in a nursery rhyme, "Eat a fairy's food, become a fairy's slave." You look around at the jolly crowd. That was just a nursery rhyme, right? Maybe it's time to return to the car park to see if Alastair is waiting for you after all.

If you would like to make your choice without reading up on fairies, go on to the next page.

If you would like a quick refresher lesson in the ways of fairies before you make your choice, turn to page 26.

Make your decision below.

*If you decide to stay with Elaine in the large
hall and risk eating the fairy feast before
continuing your search for Alastair,
turn to page 38.*

*If you decide to return above ground to look
for Alastair immediately, turn to page 54.*

FAIRY LORE

There are many theories about fairies, but it is agreed that they:

a. Are human in appearance with magical powers
b. Do not like iron and will not go near it
c. Have magical powers including flying, casting spells, and foretelling the future

The name *fairy* comes from an old French word *faerie* meaning "enchantment."

Some believe that fairies are an intelligent species similar to humans but smaller and distinctly different. It is believed that they were driven into hiding over 100 years ago by human encroachment on fairy lands worldwide as population exploded during the Industrial Revolution. Some fairy habitations are now also underground.

*Fae Person,
Example 2*

*Fae Person,
Example 1*

Others believe that fairies are angels who have committed a crime or sin. They have been forced to live in the earth realm and are quite mischievous. These fairies can change their shape at will. Some of their acts can be actually harmful. It is not known whether this is intentional or whether they do not understand how their actions affect humans.

Fairy time is different. Fairies have a hard time understanding the concept of minutes, hours, days, weeks, etc. People exposed to fairy mischief have reported time travel is one of their dark arts.

Fairies can survive without food or nourishment for long periods. When they eat, they tend to over-indulge and eat several times their body weight at a single sitting. There are reports that a human who eats fairy food becomes highly susceptible to their schemes and plans, although actual enslavement is rare.

Fae Person,
Example 3

When you are ready to go back and make your choice, turn to page 25.

"They took that cool weapon from your photograph?" Twig asks.

"Yes," you answer. "Apparently it is the key to the whole ritual. That is why Alastair gave it to me. He thought that by taking it to the British Museum it would keep it out of the hands of the ones who wanted to perform the ritual to make the land barren. These Druid guys are going to use it to perform some sort of ritual at Stonehenge in the next two days. Liandra thinks that they mean to murder people as a sacrifice to the Green Goddess."

"Who is Liandra?" Twig asks.

"She's a wood sprite, but that doesn't matter right now," you answer. "Can you get through to the police and see if they will come out to Stonehenge with me? Leave out all of the magical stuff, though."

"I'll do what I can," he says. "What happened at the museum, anyway?"

"That guy Bloom was one of them. At least that is what Alastair says."

"You head to Amesbury and I'll call the police," Twig says.

Turn to page 121.

You awake with a jerk.

"OPEN UP! OPEN UP RIGHT NOW!"

Someone is banging hard on your door. It sounds like they are about to knock it down.

"Who is it?" you demand.

"YOU ARE IN POSSESSION OF VALUABLE STOLEN PROPERTY. OPEN THIS DOOR AT ONCE!"

Stolen? Do they mean the Golden Sickle? But who even knows you have it? Did someone see Alastair hand it to you? No one followed you last night, you are certain. And no one knew where you were staying. Then it hits you: someone must have intercepted your cell phone message with the photo!

"Open up now you little bugger!"

WHOOOMP!

Whoever is outside is now throwing themselves against your door, trying to break it down. You must act quickly. Alastair warned you to guard the sickle with your life. But you thought it was a figure of speech.

If you take the sickle and escape out the window, turn to page 36.

If you decide to call the police on your cell phone, turn to page 47.

30

You decide to head straight to the British Museum. You call ahead from the taxi. Standish Bloom turns out to be Director of Ceremonial Antiquities. His assistant seems about to brush you off until you mention the Golden Sickle. He puts you on hold, and you half expect him to hang up.

"Dr. Bloom will see you immediately," he says, coming back on the line.

Your taxi pulls up in front of the British Museum. You find Bloom's office without any trouble.

"He'll be right with you," Bloom's assistant says with a smile.

You don't have to wait long. Bloom comes rushing out to meet you. "Did you bring it with you?" he asks immediately, without introducing himself.

"The sickle? Of course," you say. You are taken aback by his eagerness. "It's right here in my pack."

"Sorry, why don't you come into my office and we can have a private chat?" he says, trying to sound more friendly. "Call me Standish, by the way. Sorry for my brusque greeting."

He waves you into his inner office.

Go on to the next page.

Bloom's office is very elegant with comfortable chairs and fireplace blazing. A number of strange but interesting objects cram the shelves.

"So tell me all about it," he says, offering you a chair. "How did you come across this?"

"Last night. I had an arranged appointment with a man named Alastair Shepherd. You know him, correct?"

"Yes, very well," Bloom replies.

"I thought he was going to tell me something about the missing heelstone. I'm an amateur archaeologist. But instead he gave me this," you say.

You place the small box on Mr. Bloom's oak desk and open it. The Golden Sickle gives off a glow that makes it seem warm and alive.

"Ahh," says Dr. Bloom, with a sigh. "I've dreamt of this moment for a long, long time."

"What is it?" you ask.

"This may be the fabled Golden Sickle of the Dunedain. The Druids recorded its history."

"I thought the Druids didn't write anything down?" you ask.

Turn to page 33.

"We thought that was the case until about five years ago," Dr. Bloom says. "Then there was an interesting discovery in Wales." He pauses to look at the sickle. "I need to go get Lester. He is our best dater."

Dr. Bloom leaves the room. You stare at the sickle in the box, and pick the sickle up again to look at the intricate designs on the blade, when your cell phone rings.

"Twig?" you answer expectantly.

"Have you given him the sickle?" The voice on the other end is harsh and ragged. It's not Twig at all. "Whatever you do, don't give it to him!"

"Alastair? Are you all right?" you ask.

"No, I'm not. I was wrong to send you to Bloom. He's one of them!"

"One of whom? What are you talking about?" you reply.

"I can't explain now. You have to get out of there. Immediately. Your life is in danger. Don't give him the Golden Sickle, otherwise all is lost," he says.

"What am I supposed to do?" you cry.

"I'll email your friend…"

Then you hear a strange cry before the line goes dead.

Outside, you can hear Dr. Bloom approaching.

Turn to the next page.

"Here we are," Bloom says cheerily, rounding the corner. He is with a tall, pale man wearing a suit and tie. "Thanks so much for bringing us the sickle. We will be sure to give you full credit for the discovery! It could make you somewhat famous. Lester will take it to the lab and analyze and date it."

He reaches out to take the box with the Golden Sickle, but you stand between him and the box.

If you choose to accept Alastair's instructions and take the sickle back, turn to page 43.

If you decide to let Dr. Bloom have the sickle, turn to page 69.

36

"Hold on. I'll be right with you," you say. "Just pulling on my clothes."

"You've got fifteen seconds," the voice outside replies.

You don't have time to dress. That was a bluff. You throw your clothes into your pack and jump out the small window. It's not far to the ground and you roll when you land, breaking the blow. You are standing in some sort of parking lot behind the inn facing a low stone wall with a large field beyond. You can smell the garbage dumpster nearby. Up above, you hear the door to your room crack and break as your pursuers kick it in.

If you decide to jump into the dumpster to hide, since you have seen that several times in the movies and it always seems to work, turn to page 51.

If you decide to jump the stone wall and run for the moors, turn to page 104.

38

"It can't hurt to eat a bit of fairy food," you say. "I must admit I'm starved."

"We prefer to be called Fae these days. Fairies, Kelpies, Wee Folk—those terms are kind of old school," Elaine says.

"Right, *Fae* food then," you reply.

You and Elaine find empty seats at one of the long tables. Within seconds, plates of food appear in front of you. Every bit is delicious. You eat roast beef with Yorkshire pudding, baby asparagus with a delicious lemon butter sauce, grilled chicken with mashed potatoes, lasagna, and more mashed potatoes. Alastair seems more and more remote as you eat this wonderful feast.

After you have eaten three whole plates of food, the desserts begin to arrive. First you dig in to a piece of pecan pie with homemade vanilla ice cream. Then you accept a bowl of brown sugar-roasted bananas with chocolate sauce. You follow that with a tiny raspberry tart, and a fat slice of spice cake. Finally, you finish off with a miniature meringue swan filled with blueberry custard.

"I don't care if I do become your slave," you say to no one in particular. "This is the best meal I've ever eaten."

All the nearby fairies break out laughing, as if you've said the funniest thing in the world. One of them is about to say something, when the crystal bell rings. The whole hall quiets in an instant.

Go on to the next page.

"The queen," Elaine whispers, answering your look. "She is about to speak."

At Elaine's words, the Fae woman in the green velvet dress stands on the stairs leading to huge oak doors at the other end of the hall.

"Let us give our thanks to the cooks and the waiters!" A huge roar of thanks goes up from the assembled crowd, and you join in with enthusiasm.

"Now we are ready to pay respects to the light of the sun, on this longest day of days. But we will also bring our honor and love to the glories of the night!"

With those words, the queen proceeds to march through the oaken doors out of the dining hall. Guests fall in line behind her, and you see many take glowing torches from off the walls as they pass into a large, dark tunnel. If you have your directions straight, it leads toward Stonehenge.

Turn to the next page.

40

You hurry to follow after the queen into the tunnel. Everyone starts to sing a low tune as they march.

Sun down, sun down, moon rise, moon rise
When it drops, wise eye, wise eye!

The queen reaches the end of the tunnel. She begins to climb a set of worn stone steps without pausing. You and Elaine are not far behind. As you step out of the darkness, you realize that you are in the middle of the Stonehenge monument. You see the fading light of the end of the longest day. A honey glow makes everything seem special and full of life. You look around, but you can't see any of the police, the barricades, or the thousands of people who were in the parking lot. All that you can see is green and untouched.

You are about to ask where everything went when the Fae queen steps into the middle of the circle. Just as she does so, the sun sets. She raises her hands up as if she is making an offering. Her face is strong and beautiful in the last of the fading light. You fall to your knees along with all the others.

"We kneel to honor the Sun and the Earth," Elaine whispers. "This is the most powerful time of the year, the time when Her Majesty gets her visions."

"Visions of what?" you ask.

Before Elaine can answer, the queen lets out an anguished cry and falls to the ground, unconscious. The whole crowd gasps.

Turn to page 65.

"Just a minute," you say, scooping up the box and closing it before Dr. Bloom can get to it. You hold it close to your body. "I never said that you could have the sickle. I just wanted you to examine it and give me background on it."

"I'm afraid you just don't understand the reality of the situation," says Dr. Bloom, taking a step towards you and holding a hand out for the box. "We appreciate that you helped bring it to our attention, but all antiquities found in the United Kingdom are the property of the state. It is illegal to hold them personally."

His insincere smile irritates you. You are glad at that moment that you did not give him the sickle. "How do you know this is from the UK? Nothing I've seen has given me any proof to that effect," you say, edging toward the doorway. The tall man that you assume is "Lester" moves to block you off.

"Come now, don't be foolish!" says Bloom. "Lester, call security. Please hand over the box and we'll forget this bit of unpleasantness. If you do not, you will be dealt with as the law permits."

"Sure, I'll give it to you as soon as you return the Elgin marbles!" you shout as you duck by Dr. Bloom and rush past Lester. Both make moves to grab you, but you manage to escape. You slip out the open doorway, past the secretary and into the narrow hallway, running as fast as you can.

Turn to the next page.

"Come back! Stop that person!" you hear Bloom shout. Luckily you are not in the museum proper. There are no security guards handy. At the end of the hall, opposite the way you came in, you see a door with an emergency exit sign. You run toward it and push through. As soon as you do, the alarm sirens sound.

You are outside in a narrow alleyway. It leads into a busy street so you take off in that direction. Clutching the package tightly to your chest, you rush into the street. You almost knock someone over.

"Sorry 'bout that!" you yell over your shoulder. You were never a track star, but you hope that you can run faster than an aging antiquities specialist. You sneak a peek behind you. Good. No sign of Bloom or his sidekick. The summer streets are crowded with tourists and people out for lunch. It gives you cover. You duck into a side street and keep running.

After a few minutes you come to a small, green park. You finally stop running and put the package into your pocket. That is when you realize that you left your backpack in Bloom's office. Nothing irreplaceable is in the bag. It's lucky your cell phone and wallet are in your jacket pocket. But they'll learn your home address.

Go on to the next page.

You continue through the park and on to the nearest Tube station. You are afraid to call Twig in case they can track your cell phone. You decide to go in person.

You ride the London Underground randomly for an hour, changing trains frequently. No one seems to be on your trail. You get off at the station nearest Twig's house. As you emerge from the underground, your cell phone beeps. It's a text message.

Come to North Yorkshire asap. Train from King's Cross at 12:10. See map below. Essential that you bring package I gave you. Will explain once we meet. Do not tell anyone your plans. Please reply and confirm arrival.
    -Alastair

You look at your watch. It's 11:40. You have just enough time to catch the train from Waterloo Station if you leave immediately.

If you decide to try to catch the 12:10 to Yorkshire and call Twig from the train, turn to page 48.

If you decide to go to Twig's first, turn to page 68.

You decide to call the police, but you'll need to distract whoever is outside your door.

"I need to pull on some clothes. Just a second," you say, playing for time.

You look around. There's a heavy dresser just next to the door. With a big shove, you manage to slide it in front of the door blocking access, at least for a few moments. Then you pop into the closet to dial emergency and whisper your location.

Outside there is another *WHOOMPH!* This time the wood on the door frame cracks and the dresser bounces a half of an inch.

"Where did you say you were?" the dispatcher asks.

"The Ball and Crown," you reply. "Please come quickly."

You leave the closet and push against the dresser as the two men outside continue to try to knock down the door. It feels like you are there pushing at the dresser forever. But it's probably just two minutes when you hear a siren in the distance. The two men outside go silent. You hear a woman's voice down the hall.

"It's the cops! We've got to run. They've pulled up outside the front door."

You recognize the voice. It's Elaine the fairy!

Turn to page 53.

48

You make an impulsive decision to try to catch the train. You forward the text message to Twig, just in case you can't reach him. You reach King's Cross Station with five minutes to spare. Once the train is moving, you pull out your cell phone to examine Alastair's map. It indicates a trailhead leading to a place called "Wainstones." The nearest place is a small town called Northallerton. You call Twig again, but still no answer. You wonder what could be going on and why he still hasn't called.

You sleep on the way north, with the Golden Sickle zipped safely into your inner coat pocket.

"I'm going to the Wainstones," you tell the cabbie outside the Northallerton station. "Have you heard of it?"

"The pub?" he asks.

"No, it is supposed to be an ancient rock formation. Near the town of Great Broughton," you reply.

"Sure, I've been mountain biking up there. Hop in," he says.

Half an hour later you are climbing. The trail is steep at first. But the stone path evens out once you get up to the ridgeline of the moor. Your thoughts keep returning to Alastair's warning. What did he mean when he said that Bloom was "one of them"? A gentle breeze cools you as you hike. Despite feeling distracted, you do enjoy the scenery of peaceful small villages set against the deep green countryside.

Turn to page 50.

50

You get to the Wainstones just as the sun sets. It is a haphazard jumble of sandstone boulders. The sky glows red in the west, and you look around to see if anyone is there to meet you. You move forward into the pile of dark stones, turning on the flashlight you bought at the station. As you move between two large rocks, something hard smashes into the back of your head. Everything goes dark.

When you wake up, you are tied hand and foot with a thick rope. A gag is in your mouth. You look around which causes a sharp pain to shoot down your neck.

You are lying in the mud in what looks like a dense forest, in front of a small campfire. Dark hooded shapes move about the fire, casting flickering shadows. One holds the Golden Sickle high above his head and begins chanting.

"I'm so sorry I brought you into this," whispers a voice behind you. "I have managed to make a mess of the whole thing."

You open one eye and turn your head slightly to see who is talking. Alastair? It is hard to tell in the darkness, but his face looks like a mass of bruises and his lip is split open. Blood oozes slowly from it.

"Like I should talk to you?" you hiss. "I'm attacked by crazies for the second time in one day!"

Turn to page 56.

You decide to jump into the dumpster. It's even more disgusting than you imagined. The stink is tremendous and you sit on something squishy that slowly begins to penetrate the fabric of your pants. Yuck.

Up in your room, your pursuers call out, "Where are you, you bloomin' thief?" It sounds like they are tearing the furniture apart. Then you hear one of them hang his head out the window.

"Bugger must have jumped!" Two swift thuds follow.

Then silence. Did they knock themselves unconscious when they jumped? Should you stick your head out and look?

Turn to the next page.

52

You slowly raise your head to peer above the trash.

THWAACK!

You feel a sharp pain in your skull and everything goes dark.

Turn to page 125.

"We'll get you one of these days," a strange lilting voice says darkly through the door. "The sickle belongs to us."

Then your three assailants trot quickly down the hall.

A single drop of sweat rolls down your back, reminding you how hard you have worked to protect yourself and the strangely compelling Golden Sickle. You slump to the floor, scared and tired, and wait for the police to arrive.

In less than a minute they are there. You move the dresser back, open your door and tell them your story. Or most of it. Everyone listens attentively. A plainclothes detective asks, "Do you have stolen goods?"

"I don't believe the Golden Sickle is stolen, no. But I am not sure, to be honest," you reply.

"I think you better come back to the station, so we can get your story again, and from the beginning," the inspector says.

The End

54

"Elaine, thank you for the invitation to eat. But I promised my friend Twig I would meet Alastair. I think I better go back outside and continue to wait," you say as politely as you can.

Elaine grins mischievously. "Fairy time is different, you know," she announces. She reaches out to a passing tray of chocolate covered strawberries and pops one in her mouth.

"What is that supposed to mean? We've been here less than fifteen minutes," you answer.

"Go look for Alastair, then," she replies, skipping off. "Good luck!" She laughs in a rather snippy way and joins some friends sitting nearby.

You take one last look around the cavernous chamber, so you can sketch it later, and turn on your heels.

You nod goodbye to the fairy guards as you return to the narrow dark tunnel leading to the car park. They murmur something and exchange nervous glances, but they do not try to stop you.

"The sooner I'm back above ground, the better," you mumble.

You retrace your steps, and arrive at the oval wooden door. The guard elf is talking on a cell phone and laughing uproariously. He ignores you as you grasp the wooden handle and open the door.

Go on to the next page.

As soon as you step outside into the green field, the door slams shut behind you. That's funny. The light has changed. It looks like late afternoon.

You take a few steps forward and turn to look toward the car park. But it's gone. You run a few more feet forward. The car park and thousands of people should be in plain view. But the fields are empty. The only living thing is a horse-drawn carriage approaching on a dirt road. You wave it down.

"What happened to everyone?" you cry.

"Everyone?" The carriage stops. "I have no idea what you are talking about," the driver replies. He's dressed in an old-fashioned frock coat and top hat.

"I'm in Amesbury, right? Near the Stonehenge monument, right?" you ask.

"Right. Amesbury, England. 1844. Are you lost?" he answers.

"1844?" you reply weakly.

The End

56

"They made me call you. I didn't want to do it, but they have ways, methods, to make you do things against your will," he says. His words are quiet and a bit mushy. You think he may be missing some teeth. "I think they mean to sacrifice us to the Gods of the Green, the Gods of the Sun, and the Gods of the Stone. Again, I am so sorry."

You only half pay attention to what he says. You are focused on the small pocket knife you taped to the inside of your right thigh. Getting it without being noticed is your main problem.

"Of course, the Wainstones are a secondary focal point for the energy of the Old Ones," Alastair continues. "But Stonehenge and the Ring of Brodgar are too well-guarded now. Anyone can come to the Wainstones, though…"

Go on to the next page.

The figure with the Golden Sickle stops chanting. At least ten others join him in front of the fire. They begin to chant as well. They are all looking in your direction, but you can't see their faces within their dark hoods. You try to look like you are struggling in your sleep. You flop over and manage to get the knife in your bound hands.

"They are coming to the end of the first part," says Alastair, matter of factly. "They will all turn and bow to the Arch-Druid. That's your chance to cut your bindings. Once you start running, I'll scream and roll into the fire. That should distract them long enough for you to get away. Just head down slope. We are only a couple of miles from town and there are lots of paths. They may even give up if you get a good lead. Most Druids don't want to be caught."

You don't know what to make of this, but as soon as they kneel down, you start sawing feverishly with your little knife. Sweat runs into your eyes, and your head pounds from the earlier blow. Finally, you cut through the ropes at your feet and feel your bindings fall away.

If you decide to try and free Alastair first before escaping, turn to page 59.

If you choose to follow Alastair's plan and run away immediately, turn to page 83.

58

You repeat Antares's riddle in your head. Then it hits you.

"There are no stairs. It's a single story house," you announce.

"Right! Lucky guess!" Antares screams. First he stamps his foot on the ground. The whole mountain shakes. Then he picks up a boulder and throws it at you. *SMACK!* It lands two feet away.

"ANTARES, FAIR IS FAIR!!!" someone yells. It's Elaine.

Antares frowns. "I hate fairies," he says.

"You might hate fairies, but my friend has won the challenge. Now grant a wish," Elaine orders.

"I get a wish?" you ask. "Any wish?"

Elaine nods.

Antares is so angry, his ears have turned red. This is something you have only seen before in small babies.

"I wish I could visit Mohenjo-Daro," you announce. *ZOCEROO!*

Turn to page 102.

It's a tough choice but you decide to try to help Alastair escape. You aren't sure there's time to get to town and back with police before the Druids do something terrible. Besides, without his help just now, you doubt that you would have been able to cut yourself free without being seen. Pretending to still be bound, you roll over and begin to saw through the ropes holding his ankles together.

"Please, just get out of here. My life is forfeit anyway. They will track me down no matter where I go. You, they don't care about," he says. "They will be finished any second!"

You ignore him and concentrate on sawing the cords. At one point, you start rushing and you almost drop the knife. You force yourself to slow down, and you cut through the last bond just as the Druids get up from kneeling.

Alastair starts rolling away from the fire and you follow behind him. You try to be as quiet as possible. No one has noticed you moving yet, but you know it is just a matter of moments until they do. Once you reach the edge of the darkness away from the firelight, you try to stand. You fall face first into the mud, but you don't stop for a second. You just keep trying.

Turn to page 61.

"Hey!" someone shouts as you stumble to your feet.

You head off blindly into the darkness of the trees. At this point, there is no more that you can do for Alastair.

Your feet slip in the mud, and you crash through thick pine and spruce branches. But soon you reach a sort of farming path or logging road. You hope that the footsteps right behind you are Alastair's, but you don't waste time looking. You decide against taking the path. It's too obvious. Instead you head into the thickest part of the woods. You stumble across a small stream and up the bank on the other side.

"Downhill," Alastair whispers at a juncture a minute later. So it is him behind you. Out of the corner of your eye you catch a glimpse of flashlight beams cutting through the darkness of the night. You keep moving and hope that the noise of all the others will mask your own. Alastair is two steps behind you.

"Get down!" he hisses suddenly. "He cast a spell of Root Wrapping, we need to lie low."

"What?" you reply. But you do what he says. You lie down on the far side of the bank, next to a fallen tree. Reaching forward, you grab Alastair and bring him next to you. You see the shape of writhing snakes all around you and try to scream, but Alastair clamps his hand over your mouth first.

Turn to the next page.

62

"It's just the spell," he explains. "As long as we are clear of the roots, we'll be okay. It'll be over in a minute. Perhaps longer because we are near the Wainstones."

You are not really sure what Alastair is saying. Your heart beats in your chest. You try to keep from gasping for air. All around, the roots seem to come alive and move toward you. Taking the knife, you stab at a nearby root that is inches from your feet. It recoils as soon as you cut into it. Other roots seem to feel it! They shake loose from the binding earth and reach out towards you!

"Time to get out of here," Alastair whispers. He points to the streambed. Taking his cue, you move into the flowing water and start moving downstream.

"Get down," Alastair says, grabbing you and pulling you towards the water.

You wait as you hear people moving through the woods.

"They can't have gone far. Have the others found anything?" says a deep voice that you don't recognize.

"No sir, nothing yet," says a voice that sounds subservient.

"We'll need to get out of here if we can't find them soon. The plans are too far along to jeopardize everything now. Besides, who will believe them?" says the first voice.

Go on to the next page.

"Alastair knows too much," the second man replies. "He could prove problematic for the Grand Design if he gets through to the media. On a slow news day, he might get some attention."

"You're right, we need to find them." There's a pause. "If we don't do so soon, call everyone back to the stones. We'll perform the Death Spell once we get to the grove. Alastair shall find that leaving the Suns is not so easy as he would like to think," the first voice says.

Alastair looks at you. You can see him shaking, even in the darkness of the wood, but he remains silent. The two of you wait for a few more minutes. Then you continue down the stream. Occasionally you hear some of the Druids in the distance, but the noises get fainter as you move further away.

"What is the Death Spell?" you ask once it has been quiet for some time.

"When you become one of the Inner Circle of the Suns of Stonehenge, you are bound, both literally and figuratively, to the sacred grove. Your blood feeds the oaks. You are tied to a tree for three days without food or water," he whispers as you get to the edge of the wood. Small clouds scud across the sky and you see Alastair's face in the moonlight. "If you survive, you become part of the wood. You both give and gain strength from its deep roots."

"Yeah, but how does it work?" you say, impatient in your fear.

Turn to the next page.

64

"They need the Golden Sickle. First they cut the tree with it and then burn the scar with sacred fire. Thus the bond is broken. If that happens, the tree may survive, but the person never does. Usually the target dies immediately, but sometimes they linger. At least according to legend. I have never seen the Death Spell. Burning one of the trees in the Sacred Grove is a very drastic step."

"Let's get to the police station," you say as you run through a field of rapeseed. The warm lights of town seem close and inviting. "Maybe we can stop them before they get to the grove!"

"There is no point. I would never give up the location of the grove, even if my life depended on it. Which, I guess, it does," he says with a weak laugh. "Besides, I fear we may find enemies all around us. There is one who may be able to help us. She will at least spread the word of what they intend to do."

"Who is she?" you ask.

"Her name is Liandra. A wood sprite. She will take us both in if I ask her to."

If you decide to join Alastair on his journey to the wood sprite, turn to page 70.

If you choose to go to the police station, and bring Alastair with you, turn to page 98.

"What's happened?" you ask. Elaine shakes her head.

The fairies move quickly to help the queen. She awakens and struggles to her feet, brushing them back. "I will be perfectly fine," she says in a strong tone. She looks around the assembled fairy throng. She seems to be looking for someone. Then her eyes lock with yours and she stops. She whispers something to her minions and points in your direction. Then she departs. A nervous murmur of worry rises from the crowd when she is gone.

"This cannot be good," Elaine says with a frown.

Someone else says, "I've never seen it happen and I've been attending for 332 years!"

One of the queen's pages approaches. You feel all eyes on you as he comes near. He leans in and says in a low voice, "The queen would like to see you in her audience chamber. Please follow me, if you would be so kind."

You nod your agreement.

Turn to the next page.

The page leads you back down the stairs, through several tunnels you don't remember seeing before, and through carved wooden doors and into a small room with comfortable chairs and a roaring fire. On a table in front of the fire is a small bowl of glowing blue water. You stare into the fire for a few moments.

"The song is more than just a tradition," the queen says. You jerk around. She has entered the room without a sound. "At the setting of the solstice sun on midsummer's eve, knowledge of the future is given to the one who knows how to ask. The henge also acts as an energy vortex. It balances the forces of earth—bringing in gratitude, cleansing the greed and hate. And the balancing occurs for just a few minutes each solstice. But it is essential to our, and your, survival."

"What happened tonight?" you ask.

"I saw a terrible fate that is going to befall both the Fae and you humans. Unfortunately, the henge has fallen into such a state of disrepair that I can't find out more about the fate that threatens without getting help. What needs to be done, a Fae cannot do. So I need your help."

Go on to the next page.

"Why me?" you ask. "What can I do?"

"The henge was built by three groups: humans, giants, and the trow," the queen replies. "All three worked together to build it, long ago. I need someone to go talk to the giants or the trow to help us figure out what this oracle means."

"But why don't you go, or one of your people?"

"The truth is that we Fae have had, shall we say, moments of unpleasantness with both the giants and the trow. They would not treat our request well if one of us were to go," she says.

"I think I know what giants are," you say. "But what are trow?"

"Trow are the barrow dwellers, or hogboons. Sometimes they are called goblins, but I would not say that to their faces. They are tough, but not overly mean. We have had our conflicts through the years. Please, can you do this? I would not ask unless I truly needed help. It has to be freely done. Otherwise I would merely place you under a spell."

You feel a strange compulsion to say yes. In fact, you don't even consider refusing.

"I'll do it," you say.

"Wonderful. Would you prefer to go to the giants? Or are you more inclined to try the trow?"

*If you choose to visit the giants,
turn to page 79.*

*If you choose to go to the trow,
turn to page 87.*

68

Something feels funny to you about the text message. You decide to go to Twig's first. You can catch a later train if it's really important.

When you pull the Golden Sickle from its package twenty minutes later, you are stunned again at its incredible power.

"This might be the most amazing ancient artifact I've ever seen," Twig agrees. "It's magnificent."

You show the sickle to Twig's dad later that day. He calls a friend in the House of Lords. Before you know it, you and Twig are on the BBC, describing the strange series of events that led you to the Golden Sickle.

"No," you reply to the reporter's question. "We have never heard from the mysterious Alastair Shepherd again."

It turns out your instincts on Standish Bloom were also correct. A few discreet inquiries and Bloom and his secretary are busted as the London branch of a huge illegal antiquities ring. Bloom is sentenced to ten years in prison after a flashy trial. You think of him every time you stop by the British Museum to look at the extraordinary Golden Sickle on display, for everyone to enjoy.

The End

You hand the Golden Sickle to Dr. Bloom.

"We'll be in touch shortly when we have verified dates," he says, smiling and shaking your hand. "Thank you so much for coming by. And now I will have to excuse myself for I am due at a meeting."

His secretary ushers you out of Bloom's office. You head to Twig's house where he is disappointed not to see the sickle in person.

"I'll be keen to see what the museum thinks," he says with a sigh.

You wait a full week and hear nothing from Standish Bloom. At the end of the second week, you and Twig decide to call.

"I'm sorry," Dr. Bloom tells you. "You must be mistaken. I have never seen the Golden Sickle you mention. And I've never heard of you before in my life. Besides, any time the museum takes possession of an object, we certainly give the person in question a receipt. Good day and stop bothering me. I run a serious department!"

You and Twig are speechless. The only remaining trace of the sickle is a slightly fuzzy cell phone snapshot. You never hear from Alastair Shepherd again.

The End

"How do we get to Liandra's?" you ask.

"It isn't far. We can call a taxicab. There is a public phone up ahead. We can hide in the churchyard while we wait."

The adrenaline from your flight wears off. You shiver as you hide amidst the worn sandstone gravestones in the churchyard. Alastair makes the call. There is no sign of the other Druids. Eventually the cab comes.

"We were camping and got lost in the woods," explains Alastair when the cab driver stares at your mud-covered bodies. "We decided to spend the night indoors."

Go on to the next page.

The ride takes about an hour. You travel up and over the moors where the terrain flattens out. In the distance you can see the dark shape of the North Sea. The cabbie doesn't say anything as he drops you by the side of a dark wood. But you can tell that he has doubts about your stated plans of sleeping indoors.

"Here's my cell number, if you can't find your friend's cabin," he says before driving away into the night.

Turn to the next page.

You follow Alastair into the wood. It has a profoundly peaceful feeling.

"This is one of the oldest woods in Britain," he says, as you make your way between towering hemlocks and hickories. "Most of the trees in England have been cut down, either during wars or the Industrial Revolution. This is one of the few spots that survived all that. I came here often as a young man. That is when I met Liandra."

You reach a wetter area. Small pools of water glisten in the moonlight.

"Here we are," Alastair announces when you come to a halt about forty feet from a weeping willow. "Please let me do the talking. Wood sprites have good reason to not trust humans."

Alastair motions for you to stay. He approaches the willow and moves underneath its canopy. Several minutes later, he leans out and gestures for you to come join him.

"Welcome," a sweet voice says as you push the branches aside. "I am Liandra."

You see a small woman before you. Instead of hair, she has branches like those of her tree, but with finer leaves and stems. Her skin has both smooth yellow and rough brown bark-like parts that look like clothes.

"Hello," you reply, not sure what else to say.

"Please take something to drink," she says as she holds a hollowed-out horn towards you.

Turn to page 74.

"Thank you," you tell Liandra, accepting her offer. Alastair wears a neutral expression. You take the bowl to your lips and drink something bright, like sparkling spring water, but with no bubbles. You feel a warm glow spread through your body. The pain where your feet and hands were bound eases immediately.

"I feel much better," you say, handing the bowl back to Liandra. She passes it to Alastair, who takes a long drink.

"Now please tell me your story from the beginning," she says. "Come with me inside, and we will sit."

You follow her to the massive trunk of the willow. There is a doorway hidden inside of it. You enter a small room with a cubby bed that looks naturally grown. A stone table and stone benches are the only other furniture. Rows of gourds line the walls on stone shelves, and fragrant herbs hang in bunches from the low ceiling. It feels cozy and safe.

Alastair sits down and gives Liandra an overview of the past few hours. Then he turns to you. "I should now tell you about what has brought you into this struggle. You were merely meant to be the conduit for the transfer of the sickle, and of course spreading the truth about the ancient prophecy that the Druids have discovered. The original builders of the henges were trying to create permanent links between the powers of the sun and the moon and the powers of trees and other plants."

Go on to the next page.

"Oh!" says Liandra, leaning forward. "I knew there was a reason I didn't kill you when I met you, Alastair!"

You ignore her strange comment and ask, "How did they do that?"

Alastair continues. "Long ago before the Druids existed, there was an ancient race of people who had to make sure that the land was going to be fruitful and not barren. You will find that there are many myths and stories about the land falling into a phase where crops withered and died. These stories are based in fact, and we are about to enter another such phase. As one of the Arch-Druids of the Sacred Grove of the Suns of Stonehenge, I believed that we could stop the new barren phase from occurring. Most of the other Druids saw it as our duty to stop such a tragedy. Some thought that we could reclaim the fertility of the land and become the just arbiters of a new world filled with respect for Earth and all her generosity. The Golden Sickle is a key element to ensuring the continued fertility of the land. It can also ensure that it will remain a wasteland. It all depends upon its use. Liandra, dear, do you have any more of the wonderful sap-health drink? I am not feeling very well all of a sudden."

Turn to the next page.

You notice Alastair's face is pale and sweaty. "Looks like they made it to the sacred grove," he says, smiling wanly.

"Drink this," says Liandra, giving Alastair the stone bowl. Alastair perks up a little bit as he takes the potion.

"Listen to me," he says. His eyes are wide. "You must stop them from fulfilling the prophecy of the barren land. The Golden Sickle is the key to the ritual of renewal; it is the only way that we can keep the land fertile. They need to make the ritual sacrifice at Stonehenge before four days have passed after the solstice. If they don't then the land will continue as it is. *Arrrhh.* I can't feel my feet!"

"Take this knife," says Liandra, pressing something cold into your hands. "Go outside, and Goddess forgiving, cut some of the cattails down

by the swamp. Then, very carefully, cut out a strip of bark from the side of this tree, my heart-home. Bring both to me as quickly as you can!"

You look down at the knife. It is stone, rough-hewn, completely different than the Golden Sickle that you had been toting for the last day. Has it only been one day? Outside, you hack through a group of cattails. They fall into your hands like sheaves of wheat cut by the sharpest scythe. It takes only a moment to cut out a long strip of willow bark from the side of the massive tree. When you push the blade into the rough bark, you feel the whole tree shudder. You rush to bring the ingredients to Liandra.

"Hurry! Bring them to me!" she shouts as you return.

Turn to page 82.

"I will go to the giants," you announce.

"Good, but first you must spend the night here as my guest. The trip tomorrow will be a long one and you will need your rest," the queen replies.

The night passes quickly. The next morning Elaine knocks and announces, "I've been appointed your guide and traveling companion. Off to the giants we go!"

You leave by a different entrance that is some distance away. When you surface, you are in a beautiful valley. It must be near Amesbury, but you have never seen it before. Time passes quickly, and you never seem to tire, even though you hike the whole day long. You see cattle, sheep, and other farm animals, but never any humans or fairies. As the shadows start to lengthen, you get to the foothills of some tall mountains. They seem bigger than anything that you have ever heard about in England. The question is: are you still in England?

"We're almost there," says Elaine brightly. You see that you have come to a plateau in front of a high black cliff. Large boulders are strewn about you like children's toys in a playroom.

SMASH!

Turn to the next page.

A gigantic boulder comes crashing out of the sky and lands near you and Elaine. You gasp and turn to look up. Another boulder is coming down from the sky, and you jump out of the way, grabbing Elaine just in time.

"You must play the game! What you choose? Brain or brawn?" a huge voice bellows down from on top of the cliff. "Fairy stay back, or you get smushed!"

Go on to the next page.

"It really is a giant!" you hiss at Elaine. "Or how could it throw that thing?"

She nods brightly.

"His name is Antares," she says.

"What does he want?"

"You need to pass some sort of test. Giants love tests. I would guess he proposes a contest where you either battle it with your wits or with your strength," Elaine replies. Her cheerful attitude is getting on your nerves.

"What should I do?" you whisper. Elaine bites her lip, thinking.

"Well, giants are known for their strength, not their smarts, but I doubt this is going to be easy either way."

"Brave little hoo-man, come up and battle Antares!"

Turn to page 90.

Liandra takes the cattails and willow bark from you. Then she puts her hand out urgently, like a surgeon demanding a scalpel.

You hand her the stone knife. She stabs downward, with a violent, sudden motion, and slashes Alastair from his throat to his belly button. She cuts through the rough cloth of his muddy, gray robe, but only lightly scores the flesh underneath. Red blood wells up from the cut, and you hear a moan from Alastair.

Next, she pushes the cattails into the length of the wound. Carefully, she takes the strip of willow bark and places it over the incision that she had recently cut open. This seals the cattails within.

"That should keep him alive until you get there," she says, collapsing over Alastair's inert body. He looks dead.

"Get where?" you ask, shouting again.

"Wherever you need to go to save him, of course, and the land. Although that might be two different places. I will be able to keep him alive for a short while. A few days at most."

"Do you know where the Sacred Grove is?" you ask Liandra.

"Of course," she says looking at you as if you should know better. "I am a wood sprite. All groves, sacred or not, are known to us."

If you decide that the best chance to find and stop the Druids is to go to Stonehenge, turn to page 118.

If you choose to go to the Sacred Grove, turn to page 126.

"I'll be back!" you whisper as you run into the night. It is difficult to see in the darkness after being near the fire light. Tree branches hit your face as you stumble through the woods. In the background, you hear someone screaming. You fear that Alastair might have been serious about rolling into the fire as a distraction. You can feel the small bulge of your cell phone in your back pocket, but you can't reach it because your hands are still bound. It would be much easier if you could simply call the police.

You keep running and eventually, you reach a wider path. The moonlight between cloud breaks lets you see where you are going. The path leads to the road and parking area near the trailhead. The parking lot is empty, so you start jogging down the road. As soon as you see a set of headlights coming your way, you step into the middle of the road and start hopping up and down to get the driver's attention.

"Help me!" you plead as the car slows to a stop. The woman behind the wheel looks at you for a moment and then rolls down her window.

"What's happened?" she asks, politely but warily.

"I've been kidnapped but I escaped. They still have my friend. Please get me to the police!"

Turn to the next page.

84

"Okay, hop in," she says.

Once at the police station, you tell your story as quickly as possible. They agree to send out a team to check on your story. You are doubtful that the Druids will still be there, but you have to try for Alastair's sake.

As you feared, there is no sign of anything at the Wainstones besides the remains of a campfire and lots of muddy footprints. The police take you seriously, and they take pictures of the scene. They collect mud samples for testing. But there is not much that they can do due to the lack of evidence or suspects. They recommend that you seek medical treatment, but besides some bumps and bruises, you feel all right.

"I'll just spend the night at a hotel, and head back to London tomorrow," you say.

You toss and turn all night. Finally, at dawn, you sleep. You are checking out in the late morning when your cell phone rings. It's the police.

Turn to page 111.

"I choose brain," you say, trying not to sound nervous.

"Brains? Not brawn? Why? You think I'm DUMB?" Antares bellows.

"No," you say. "I just think brains is my only chance. I'm not a good brawn candidate."

You squeeze your bicep, puny compared to Antares, as proof.

"Riddle!" Antares booms.

"Riddle?" you ask.

"You must answer riddle," he says gruffly.

"Right, I get it," you say.

Antares strokes his chin and thinks. "OK," he finally says. "Here's the riddle." He clears his throat and begins:

"There is green single story house. Everything in it is green. Doors are green, windows are green, walls are green."

"Yes, and…?" you ask.

"What color are the stairs?" Antares crosses his arms on his chest proudly, as if he's the world's reigning genius.

If you say green, turn to the next page.

*If you try to think of another answer,
turn to page 58.*

86

"The stairs would be green too," you announce.

The minute the words are out of your mouth, Antares shrieks with glee.

"I win! I win! I win!" he booms.

"Would you mind explaining?" you reply. You are not amused.

"No stairs in single story HOUSE!!"

You get a sinking feeling in your stomach. You missed that word. Antares is right.

"So you win. Now what?" you ask.

"Now you are Antares's slave for next fifty years. Antares thirsty. Go get water now!"

"Are you kidding? Fifty years?"

Antares picks up a boulder and throws it at you. *THWACK!* It misses by inches. "NOW!"

"Okay, okay," you say, jumping to your feet. "I'm going."

You frantically scan the horizon for Elaine, but she is nowhere in sight.

The End

"I would like to try the trow, Your Majesty," you say.

"Hobgoblins," she says, nodding at your decision in agreement. "The trow inhabit the human side," she adds. "Elaine can take you. Be careful of their tricks."

"I will," you promise.

Elaine leads you down a complicated series of tunnels. You finally reach another oval wooden door and push through to the outside. You come out about a quarter mile from Stonehenge, right near the road to Amesbury. In the distance you can hear the music and singing of the solstice celebration.

"Trow like this area for some reason," Elaine explains.

Ten feet away, a van has pulled over to the side of the road. It's filled with some people wearing kilts and painted blue. The engine turns over and over, but won't catch.

"Sure sign of trow nearby," Elaine whispers, pointing. "They love to play tricks with car engines."

You nod as if this is perfectly normal information.

"Here, let me try calling them," she says. Elaine begins whistling, a long low whistle.

Something rustles in the tall grasses nearby. You spot a quick flash of dark fur.

Turn to the next page.

88

Elaine stomps over and reaches down. She pulls up a small creature, no bigger than two feet tall, covered in brown fur. It has no nose.

"Found one!" she announces, holding him up. The trow thrashes wildly and hisses.

"That's a hobgoblin?" you ask.

When you say the word, the trow begins to squeal and shake his fists at you.

"Excuse me, I meant trow," you say.

"That's more like it," the short figure says.

"You speak English?" you ask.

"Every 'gob does," is the quick reply. "It's our second language. Used it to help translate the human speech when we built the henge. Back then giants didn't know a word of it."

"That's why we came to find you," you say. "It's about Stonehenge. I have a question from the fairy queen."

"What? She having trouble with her visions again?" the trow asks. With this, he lets out a guffaw.

Turn to page 96.

90

You and Elaine start to go up the narrow trail that leads switchback up the cliff.

SMASH! Another boulder comes down.

"Leave, fairy, or you get smushed!" Antares booms.

"I guess I have to wait here," Elaine says with a little smile. "Besides, if things get too crazy up top, I can always fly up to give you a hand." She flutters her wings with the last comment, before skipping away down the hill.

Just getting to the top of the cliff wears you out. You start to think that Elaine's presence had something to do with you not getting tired earlier. Anyway, you are puffing when you get to the top.

Go on to the next page.

You look around. All you see are large piles of boulders like the ones that had just almost squished you below. Then one of the boulders on top of a pile opens its mouth and starts to speak.

"Good," it says, splitting wide. A rock shape directly in front of you suddenly melts into the figure of a giant man. He is as tall as a two-story house. His skin is gray like the rock around you. Antares's hair is thick and grows out of his head like clumps of moss.

"So? What you choose? Brain or brawn?" The voice is so loud and deep you can feel it in your bones. "Make choice. Stay or go. Smash or run. Brain or brawn."

If you decide to accept the giant's challenge to a test of brains, turn to page 85.

If you choose to challenge the giant in a test of strength, turn to page 93.

93

"I will take the challenge of brawn!" you shout.

A long and loud laugh is the immediate reply. Antares's face splits into a wide grin. "Since you choose brawn, you get to pick. If you chose brain..." he trails off. You suspect that he may be a bit smarter than his simple speech indicates.

"What kind of game do we play?" you say, stalling for time.

"Your choice," Antares answers. "But it must be brawn, not brain." As he says this he stands up and stretches out his arms. They are massive compared to anything normal or human, but thin compared to his legs and trunk. His head looks oddly small perched atop such an enormous body. He picks up an uprooted tree trunk, and starts pushing the boulders around with it. One of the boulders hits another and the two crack apart like giant billiard balls.

"Hey, Antares, how about this for a game!" you shout. "I'm going to do a handstand; do you know what that is?"

"Nope, you go ahead. But if it not brawn, you get smashed," he says laughing. You hope this is a giant joke.

Taking a deep breath, you get into position to try your trick. You learned how to do a handstand when you were little and you have always practiced walking around on your hands. You get up a little unsteadily, as you are tired from the long hike and you are also nervous in front of the giant.

Turn to the next page.

"Okay, watch this," you grunt. With extreme effort, you manage to do one upside down pushup. Then you topple over, panting and with your face purple. *It must be strength from adrenaline*, you think.

"Your turn!" you yell.

Antares looks at you and closes one eye. You can't tell if he is sizing you up for a smack with the tree or if he is winking at you.

"Least you didn't say you were going to lift up the world," he mutters. Antares awkwardly squats and puts his head down. You feel the earth shake every time he moves. He sets up properly, and rests his knees on the bottom of his upper arms. But as soon as he extends his legs, he topples over. He tries again, and a third time. He never manages to get his feet into the air, let alone into a full handstand.

"Not sure that is all brawn," Antares says finally, puffing like the west wind. "But you won fair and square. No tricks either."

"I don't think you are as dumb as you want people to think," you say boldly.

"Maybe," he laughs. "I think cousin Titanos would be able to do your handstand. Maybe I'll learn so no one else can do it to me again. Why did the Fae send you?"

"Their queen saw a foretelling of doom at the solstice last night. But her vision cut short. The henge energy is clogged. She thought the original builders might know how to fix it. She needs to see what happens."

Go on to the next page.

"I don't know about hoo-man Stonehenge. I'm too young. But I know where the REAL giants' henge is. We could take a look at that and see if that helps you. Our henge isn't some itty-bitty human henge, this is a real giant henge. Or…"

"Or what?" you ask.

"I also know where Merlin lives," Antares says slyly. "He hasn't been around much lately. But he was supposed to be the one who helped us to design the henges. We did the heavy lifting and the trow did the finish work. Not sure what we needed you humans for, but maybe they counted Merlin as a human. Even though he isn't really.

"I will take you to either one. Which will it be?" he asks.

If you want to look for Merlin to find out the secrets of how the henges were built, turn to page 105.

If you decide to look at the giants' henge for clues on how to fix the human Stonehenge, turn to page 109.

96

"Considering the future of the planet might hang in the balance, is laughter appropriate?" you ask.

"She has the same trouble every year. Ever since the stones fell over and the current humans put them back up the wrong way. Planet has been out of balance ever since," the trow says. "Plain and simple."

"What can she do?" you ask.

"Nothing, except put them back the right way," the trow answers.

"What's the right way?"

"You've got to check the plans," the trow replies.

"Where are they?" you ask.

Go on to the next page.

"Can't tell you. That's a trow secret. And from secrets we get our power. But I'll give you a hint. Stonehenge is a relative of the labyrinths in Sweden. Look at those for clues. Now goodbye."

"Labyrinths in Sweden?"

The trow takes two steps back and begins to spin. Within seconds he has drilled himself into the earth. All that is left is a small mound of fresh dirt.

You turn to Elaine. "This could take a while. Sweden is pretty far away."

"We'll be here! Waiting," Elaine says. She makes a deep curtsy and prances off. A few hours later, you return to London to tell Twig your strange adventures. You decide to travel to Sweden to investigate the trow's idea. Within a year, you and Twig are famous worldwide for unlocking important secrets of Stonehenge.

The End

98

"You're coming with me," you tell Alastair, whispering fiercely. "You got me into this crazy situation. And I'm not going to be the only one telling the story. Besides, you know a lot more about the Suns of Stonehenge, Mr. Arch-Druid."

Alastair sighs and says, "Very well then, I suppose I did get you into this mess. At least they can laugh and disbelieve two of us instead of one."

You continue on until you reach a small town with a pub.

"Please, I need to talk to a policeman. Can you help me?" you ask the barkeep.

"You okay?" he asks you. "We don't have a local station here, the closest one is two towns away, but I'll call them for you. What happened?"

"It's a long story," you say. "Can you please just call? Tell them it is urgent."

Alastair orders some food and two ginger ales while you wait for the police to arrive. The events of just a few hours ago seem unreal in the warmth and noise of the pub. The door to the pub opens. You hope that it is the police, but two ordinary men walk in the door.

Turn to page 100.

100

Alastair kicks your foot under the table. "That's George and Harry!" he hisses. "They are two of the Inner Circle. They were at the Wainstones tonight!"

As he says this, the two look over at your table. The taller, meaner-looking one on the left grabs his partner and motions towards you.

Standing up abruptly, you knock over the small, round table that you were sitting at for diversion. "Come on! Let's go," you tell Alastair, grabbing at him. He is already up and moving towards the side exit.

Just then, you see flashing blue lights through the front window of the pub. George and Harry, who had started moving toward you, stop, look at each other and calmly walk out the front door. You stop and wait to see what will happen.

"Come on, let's go," says Alastair. "I have a bad feeling about this!"

"No, the cops are here," you say, standing still. "I'm not going outside now!"

Seconds later the two police officers enter the pub. One is a tall man with dark hair, while the other is a shorter woman with auburn hair. They look at the bartender, who then points in your direction. They move over to where you are standing and each one grabs one of your and Alastair's arms.

"Hey!" you cry.

Go on to the next page.

"The men you want just left! You passed them on the way in!"

"Come along, then," says the woman, not unkindly. "Let's go have a chat."

"But you're letting the kidnappers get away!" you cry.

"I think we have the kidnapper right here," says the female officer, pointing to Alastair.

The police take you to the station and put you and Alastair in separate interrogation rooms. You keep telling them how you were taken by the group of Druids and almost sacrificed, but they don't believe you. Somehow, they think Alastair had kidnapped you and brainwashed you into believing that others were out to get you. They bring up your flight from the British Museum as proof that you are part of the problem.

"But we called you!" you shout more than once.

"We were already on our way," the woman replies. "We got the call from headquarters to look for you in Great Broughton hours before you were spotted in the pub!" After they are done talking to you, they have you admitted to the psychiatric ward of a nearby hospital.

After a day and a half, Twig manages to get you released from the psychiatric ward. You learn that Alastair has allegedly "escaped" from police custody. You have your doubts, but you never see him or hear of the Golden Sickle again.

Months later you think of him when a drought kills the entire Russian wheat harvest…

The End

102

A wave of freezing cold passes over you and you pass out.

Or you think you pass out.

When you open your eyes, you are staring at the magnificent ancient city of Mohenjo-Daro from the ancient Indus civilization. It is one of the greatest archaeological sites in the world.

"Wow!" you say to no one.

You look around. The site is empty.

How are you going to get yourself out of this one?

You fish your cell phone out of your pack, and dial Twig.

The End

104

You jump the low stone wall at the back of the parking area and run into the field behind. There is a hill 200 yards away with some rock outcroppings on top. Perhaps you can hide there. You decide to head toward it.

The grass is wet and the air is immediately cooler as you run. You can hear your pursuers back at the inn. They sound like they are breaking apart the furniture in your room.

The mist gets thicker as you run. The hill up ahead becomes harder to see. Suddenly you have to stop. You can't see anything, behind or ahead. It's as if you have landed in the middle of a thick cloud.

It's then you hear the whisper, "The curse of the Golden Sickle is old and deep. You are doomed to run in the fog until next year's solstice."

"Who said that?" you cry.

Your only answer is the howling wind on the empty foggy moors.

The End

"Off to Merlin's cave," says Antares, shouting the last word. "We'll see if we can scout up the old trickster. He spreads rumors that he's dead, ya know. Keeps 'em from coming around so much." Antares lays his hand out on the ground in front of you as an invitation. "Hop on for ride. Too far for even strong hoo-man."

You take a gulp and step into the palm of his hand. His rough hand feels like the wooden planks of an old ship. But Antares picks you up with supreme gentleness and places you into the lining of his backpack. It is dark and soft and warm in Antares's backpack. It feels like a nest of sheep skins. As you drift off to sleep, you wonder if Elaine is following after you.

Turn to page 107.

When Antares comes to a stop with an abrupt jolt, dawn is breaking in the east. "Here be the cave," he says as he fishes you out of the pack. Light streams into the opening of a dark cave so large that it makes Antares seem small. The land around is rocky, with no plants growing, but inside the cave you hear the drips and gurgles of running water.

"Merlin's home," says Antares.

"How can you tell?" you ask.

"Can feel it," he replies cryptically.

Turn to the next page.

108

Antares strides forward and you follow.

"You sure you know where you are going?" you ask after you have been dropping deeper and deeper into the earth but still see no signs of life.

"Sure," says Antares confidently. "It's just a bit further."

You pass crystal soda straws, stalactites, stalagmites, and other rock formations. After a while, a path of crushed stone becomes obvious and you start to feel better about the direction that you are going.

"Uh-oh," grunts Antares. Your heart jumps.

"What?" you ask as you see the body frozen in the crystal rock before you. The figure frozen within the rock is an older man with a calm expression on his face. *It is Merlin*, you think. He looks accepting and kind. Then you notice all the other chunks of rock behind him, and none of them look accepting. Their faces are held in constant and static terror as they try and stop the final blow from falling.

You turn around and hear a sweet female voice. It is not human, but you can understand it.

"The fools always come, like crows to rancid meat."

You feel your feet turning to crystal and you try to scream. The last thing you hear is the sound of Elaine yelling your name as she flies into the cave.

The End

"Let's try the giants' henge," you announce.

"Good choice. I haven't been to the Gyytnhenge in a long time," says Antares.

With that, he picks you up and puts you on his shoulder. You grab onto something and you can't tell if it is some sort of thick shirt or a big fold of skin. You clutch it desperately. Whatever it is, it could use a wash.

You travel for a few hours this way. The landscape changes from barren and rocky to green, rolling and lush. You seem to be steadily descending. It looks like England, but without people. You spot a few musk ox grazing. In the far distance you think you see people working a farm. There are no cities or towns anywhere. Finally you reach an enormous flat plain, green as far as the eye can see.

"There it is," says Antares, pointing.

"Those black specks?" you ask.

"Just wait," he answers.

Turn to the next page.

110

It takes you and Antares almost an hour more to reach Gyytnhenge. And he is right. Up close, it is awesome and enormous. There are three rings of stones. The smallest outer stones are at least thirty feet tall. The inner henge contains stones that are at least four stories high. The stones are staggered so that it is hard to see into the center of Gyytnhenge. But you think you spot a fire burning.

The only other marker is a small stone, smaller than Antares but twice as tall as you, placed some distance away from the three circles, but lining up with the center.

Without warning, Antares picks you up and places you on the ground. He drops to one knee and bows his head.

"I pray to the guides and masters, and children of all worlds, to guide me forward and bring wisdom, healing, and balance," he whispers hoarsely. "I humbly request entry into the henge."

"Hello Antares," a voice calls out from inside the circles.

Turn to page 112.

"A man matching the description of your friend was found walking along the cliffs near the North Sea. That's about an hour from here. We wonder if you could come down and identify him?" they inquire.

When you get to the police station, you immediately recognize Alastair. He stinks and mumbles to himself. He wears nothing but his undershorts. He looks at you intently but there is no recognition in his eyes.

"Two Flap-Jacks in the morning. Right as rain. Rain or shine. Two. Always two. Or no good for you!"

"Alastair, it's me, do you recognize me?"

He nods vigorously. "Friar Tuck always ate six. Robin didn't like that, but Maid Marian took pity on the holy man and would give him a couple extra."

"Something has obviously happened to him," the police officer says. "He'll need some sort of help. Shall I call a cab for you to take him home?"

You realize you have no idea where Alastair lives. When you finally reach Twig you discover that neither does he.

"He just contacted me out of the blue," Twig says.

He ends up arranging for round the clock nursing for Alastair at his house in London. Even then it takes Alastair a full month before he regains his senses. He can't tell you anything more about that night at the Wainstones. Somehow, he does have a feeling that the Druids' plans were disrupted, but he is not sure how.

The End

112

Antares's bowed head jerks up. "Freya?" Antares says in wonder.

A tall elderly woman steps from behind one of the stones. She is dressed in long purple robes, with gold and jewels along the hem and sleeves. Her long silver hair reaches to her waist in a thick braid.

"Yes, it's me. I haven't seen you since you and your brother were caught stealing hogboon magic at the last Concurrence. That must be almost forty years ago. What brings you here today?"

Antares turns a bit red when the old woman mentions his mischief. You can't imagine getting into so much trouble that it was remembered forty years later!

"I had no idea you would be working magic at this time of year, my Lady, or else I would never have brought a guest," he says, giving you a furtive glance. "Much less a hoo-man."

"I'm not performing magic, Antares, just energy clearing, so it's all right. But it's strange to see a hoo-man here," she replies. She turns her eyes on you. You can almost feel the energy beam out of them straight into your chest. You feel a deep shiver.

"What brings you here and how can I help?" Freya asks in a commanding voice.

"Well, I, uh, I, well, uh…"

Turn to page 114.

"The Fae queen sent the youngster," Antares says. "She had a dark vision of the future on the solstice, but the hoo-man henge wasn't supplying her the full picture. So she sent this one as an ambassador to try to find out what is coming."

"And to find out why the henge won't work," you pipe in.

Freya sighs a deep sigh. She gives you a long look.

"There are several problems," she finally states. "Let us go sit inside by the fire."

You follow her into the henge and sit down on a low stone bench next to the burning embers. Antares follows but is too big for the bench, so he sits on the earth just behind. For several minutes no one talks. You watch the flames lick the burning logs. Finally Freya speaks.

"These henges, Gyytnhenge and Stonehenge, were built as energy vortexes, portals to the universe where energy imbalance could be righted, where the energy of allowing could bathe the forces of resistance," she begins. "This was needed because of the nature of thought."

You nod, even though you aren't sure you completely understand.

"You see, thoughts are things. Most do not understand this well enough, and humans do not understand this much at all."

Go on to the next page.

"When a person has a thought, the energy of that thought hangs there in space. The thought does not necessarily occur, unless your power is very strong. Most thoughts just hang there, waiting for like thoughts to bind with. Enough bad thoughts bind together, and eventually the bad thing—the same thought of many persons—actually happens on the physical realm.

"The henges were set up by the Guides to help remedy this and to clear away the bad energy, until the inhabitants of Earth and Parallel Earth could understand this more completely, until they learned to train their minds and thoughts in a more positive direction."

You nod. You kind of get it. You definitely want to talk to Twig about it.

"At Stonehenge, things were going forward for the most part, and improving, until someone moved the heelstone."

The heelstone! you think.

"Like that, there," she says, pointing to the lone henge in the distance, outside the rings. "Moving the heelstone broke the energetic circle. The portal became clogged."

"So to restore the power of Stonehenge, the heelstone must be returned?" you ask.

Turn to the next page.

116

"Yes, and hoo-mans must learn how their thoughts become things," Freya says. "Good thoughts yield good things. The future, no matter how dark it seems, can always change, as long as the thoughts change."

She stands as if she is finished. "It is time for you to go back. You have work to do," she states. She points at you with her right thumb. You feel heat in your chest that spreads to your arms and legs. A bolt of tingling passes through your entire body and for a snap instant everything goes dark.

Go on to the next page.

When you wake up you are lying on your back in a green field. You sit up. In the distance you see the car park, the road just beyond and then Stonehenge in the distance. The sun is rising in the East behind you. You are sitting in a small depression in the earth. And it hits you: you've landed in the spot where the heelstone once stood.

Where's Twig? You've got work to do!

The End

118

"Just do your best to keep him alive, Liandra," you say. "Right now I must go to Stonehenge to prevent them from performing the ritual that Alastair described earlier!"

"You know what ritual he was talking about?" she asks.

"No," you say. "But I have to stop them!"

"The Druids have many rituals, many ways of appealing to the powers of the Green, the powers of the Goddess, but I think Alastair was talking about human sacrifice. And on a grand scale."

"Well, they were already going to sacrifice Alastair and me, so I wouldn't be surprised by anything at this point. Where is the nearest train station?" you ask.

"I don't know," she replies. "I know where all the groves are, but I have never been to a train station. Is that where they make cars? I have seen cars."

"No," you say, smiling in spite of yourself. "Don't worry, I'll find my way to one soon enough. Thank you for all of your help! Take good care of Alastair."

"I will," she says. "Take this with you. It may help."

Go on to the next page.

She hands you a long willow branch. Sap oozes from the freshly cut end.

"What will I use this for?" you ask.

"It will provide power to you if you do find the other Druids," she tells you. "What they are planning is wrong, otherwise I would not help you, no matter how much I like Alastair. To make the land barren is not good, even if you humans are foolish and are doing the job by yourselves anyway. The power of the Green will not settle down easily, so you may be able to disrupt their plans."

"I'll do my best," you say, heading out of the tree home. You tie the branch around your waist, under your shirt.

Getting back to the road seems to take longer than it did to get into the wood the night before. You decide to try Twig again on your cell phone.

"Twig!" you cry when he answers on the first ring. "Where have you been?"

"Medical complications," he replies. You think you hear him wince. "What's happening?"

"It's a long story," you say. "I don't want to be dramatic, but lives are at stake. Alastair, the guy you had me meet, is in some sort of magical coma, and there are a bunch of crazy Druids who want to send the land into a time of barrenness. They took the Golden Sickle."

Turn to page 28.

Twelve hours later, you are met at the Amesbury train station by a uniformed policeman. His name is Sergeant Woodly, and he drives with you to the monument site beyond Amesbury, sirens blaring.

"Someone's gone in there," he says. "They have some sort of barrier that is keeping us all out right now. I've never seen anything like it before in my life. We're getting a 'copter in right away."

A glowing green dome covers the area all around the monument, but you can still see the stones and figures moving among them. You move forward and touch it with your hand. It is hard and unyielding, but warm, like moss heated by the summer sun. You feel a twitching sensation at your waist, and you remember the willow branch that Liandra gave you that morning.

"Watch this," you tell the Sergeant, hoping that something good will happen. Taking the willow switch from around your waist, you point it at the glowing wall. Where the tip of the willow switch touches it, the green of the barrier turns to the same orange as the doorway into Liandra's home. You put your hand out, and it goes through the barrier as if it were not there.

"Follow me," you say. "I don't know what we will find in there, but I think they mean to do a human sacrifice."

Turn to the next page.

122

You enter the monument area through the orange doorway that you have created and you cautiously creep up to the outer ring of standing stones. This is the first time you have been this close to Stonehenge, and you feel the power of this ancient site. Deep sounds of chanting seem to make the stones around you vibrate in tune with the chants.

"There is the leader," you whisper, pointing at a tall, hooded figure standing in the middle of the inner circle. On top of each of the trilithons, the stones set sideways on top of two supporting stones, stand two Druids with a bound prisoner between them. You see that they have tied a rope around the neck of each, and that the other end is tied to the stone they are standing on.

Go on to the next page.

"They are using the stones as gallows!" you tell Sergeant Woodly. "We have to stop them now!"

You rush forward, brandishing the willow switch like a sword. Only the leader is down on the ground, and he is holding the Golden Sickle high in the fading light of the sun. Slashing at his hand, you hit the Golden Sickle with the willow switch. A flash of golden light explodes as soon as the two touch. Everyone is thrown down from the force of the explosion of light.

By the time you stumble to your feet, the rest of the policemen have arrived. The Druids who were on top of the stones scramble to escape, but they are all captured quickly. The leader lies motionless on the ground. You pass out and fall gently to the green grass.

Turn to page 127.

You are awakened by the bright light.

"Blimey!" someone yells. "There's a kid in the dumpster!"

You look around, squinting in the sudden bright sun. You're in a dumpster all right. You are surrounded by garbage and a rotten smell. What are you doing here?

Two young men dressed in chef's whites reach in to help you out.

"What are you doing in the dumpster?" one asks.

"Too much partying at the henge last night, eh?" the other asks.

"Henge? What henge? What are you talking about?" you answer.

Your head throbs and you gingerly feel a lump the size of two eggs.

"Stonehenge is what henge," the first one replies. "Where are you from anyway?"

You try to think.

"I don't have any idea," you reply, feeling flustered. "I've hurt my head."

"I'll say," the second chef replies.

They take you straight to the hospital. It's two more weeks before you can remember your name. Any memory of events of the previous night, along with your backpack, and the Golden Sickle, are gone forever...

The End

Liandra tells you how to get to the Sacred Grove. Her instructions are vague, strange, and dependent on natural features that you don't know. Eventually you figure out that she is referring to The Royal Forest of Dean in Gloucester after she draws a map.

It takes you all day to make it to Gloucester, but you enter the forest before the last light disappears. You walk through the tall trees, looking at the sculptures that line the main trail. A stone fish seems to leap into the pond at Mallard's pike, and they all have a slightly sinister appearance. As you go deeper into the forest, the world around you gets darker.

"Where is the grove?" you ask yourself, wondering if you are anywhere near it.

"Just ahead," replies a voice to the left of you. A tall, dark figure in a hooded robe steps towards you. "Thank you for coming to us. It saves us the trouble of tracking you down."

The End

You wake up in a hospital room in London. Twig is there in a wheelchair. The police come into your room every few hours to talk to you about what happened. No one believes you when you tell them what actually happened, but you don't care. They keep telling you that you are a hero, though. It seems you stopped the Druids before they could complete the ritual, for the land and its crops are thriving in the warm summer weather.

"You have a letter," a nurse tells you late on your second day at the hospital. "It's a little strange," she says as she hands it to you.

The letter is made from birch bark, and the ink seems like it is berry juice, or maybe even blood.

"Alastair died last night," it starts. "There was nothing more I could do for him. Please visit when you wish. —Liandra."

The End

ABOUT THE ARTISTS

Cover Artist: Wes Louie was born and raised in Los Angeles, where he grew up drawing. He attended Pasadena City College, where he made a lot of great friends and contacts, and then the Art Center. Wes majored in illustration, but also took classes in industrial design and entertainment. He has been working in the entertainment industry since 1998 in a variety of fields.

Illustrator: Vladimir Semionov was born in August 1964 in the Republic of Moldavia, of the former USSR. He is a graduate of the Fine Arts Collegium in Kishinev, Moldavia, as well as the Fine Arts Academy of Romania, where he majored in graphics and painting, respectively. He has exhibitions all over the world, in places like Japan and Switzerland, and is currently the Art Director of the SEM&BL Animnacompany animation studio in Bucharest, Romania.

ABOUT THE AUTHOR

R. A. Montgomery attended Hopkins Grammar School, Williston-Northampton School and Williams College where he graduated in 1958. Montgomery was an adventurer all his life, climbing mountains in the Himalaya, skiing throughout Europe, and scuba-diving wherever he could. His interests included education, macro-economics, geo-politics, mythology, history, mystery novels, and music. He wrote his first interactive book, *Journey Under the Sea*, in 1976 and published it under the series name *The Adventures of You*. A few years later Bantam Books bought this book and gave Montgomery a contract for five more, to inaugurate their new children's publishing division. Bantam renamed the series *Choose Your Own Adventure* and a publishing phenomenon was born. The series has sold more than 265 million copies in over forty languages.

For games, activities, and other fun stuff, or to write to Chooseco, visit us online at CYOA.com

The History of Gamebooks

Although the *Choose Your Own Adventure*® series, first published in 1976, may be the best known example of gamebooks, it was not the first. In 1941, the legendary Argentine writer Jorge

Luis Borges published *Examen de la obra de Herbert Quain* or *An Examination of the Work of Herbert Quain,* a short story that contained three parts and nine endings. He followed that with his better known work, *El jardín de senderos que se bifurcan,* or *The Garden of Forking Paths,* a novel about a writer lost in a garden maze that had multiple story lines and endings.

Jorge Luis Borges

More than 20 years later, in 1964, another famous Argentine writer, Julio Cortázar, published a novel called *Rayuela* or *Hopscotch.* This book was composed of 155 "chapters" and the reader could make

Julio Cortázar

their way through a number of different "novels" depending on choices they made. At the same time, French author Raymond Queneau wrote an interactive story entitled *Un conte à votre façon,* or *A Story As You Like It.*

Early in the 1970s, a popular series for children called *Trackers* was published in the UK that contained multiple choices and endings. In 1976,

Journey Under the Sea,
1st Edition

R. A. Montgomery wrote and published the first gamebook for young adults: *Journey Under the Sea* under the series name *The Adventures of You*. This was changed to *Choose Your Own Adventure* by Bantam Books when they published this and five others to launch the series in 1979. The success of CYOA spawned many imitators and the term gamebooks came into use to refer to any books that utilized the second person "you" to tell a story using multiple choices and endings.

Montgomery said in an interview in 2013: "This wasn't traditional literature. The *New York Times* children's book reviewer called *Choose Your Own Adventure* a literary movement. Indeed it was. The most important thing for me has always been to get kids reading. It's not the format, it's not even the writing. The reading happened because kids were in the driver's seat. They were the mountain climber, they were the doctor, they were the deep-sea explorer. They made choices, and so they read. There were people who expressed the feeling that nonlinear literature wasn't 'normal.' But interactive books have a long history, going back 70 years."

Young R. A. Montgomery

Choose Your Own Adventure Timeline

1977 – R. A. Montgomery writes *Journey Under the Sea* under the pen name Robert Mountain. It is published by Vermont Crossroads Press along with the title *Sugar Cane Island* under the series name *The Adventures of You*.

1979 – Montgomery brings his book series to New York where it is rejected by 14 publishers before being purchased by Bantam Books for the brand new children's division. The new series is renamed *Choose Your Own Adventure*.

1980 – *Space and Beyond* initial sales are slow until Bantam seeds libraries across the U. S. with 100,000 free copies.

1983 – CYOA sales reach ten million units of the first 14 titles.

1984 – For a six week period, 9 spots of the top 15 books on the Waldenbooks Children's Bestsellers list belong to CYOA. *Choose* dominates the list throughout the 1980s.

1989 – Ten years after its original publication, over 150 CYOA titles have been published.

1990 – R. A. Montgomery publishes the *TRIO* series with Bantam, a six-book series that draws inspiration from future worlds in CYOA titles *Escape* and *Beyond Escape*.

1992 – ABC TV adapts Shannon Gilligan's CYOA title *The Case of the Silk King* as a made-for-TV movie. It is set in Thailand and stars Pat Morita, Soleil Moon Frye and Chad Allen.

1995 – A horror trend emerges in the children's book market, and Bantam launches *Choose Your Own Nightmare*, a series of shorter CYOA titles focused on creepy themes. The subseries is translated into several languages and converted to DVD and computer games.

1998 – Bantam licenses property from *Star Wars* to release *Choose Your Own Star Wars Adventures*. The 3-book series features traditional CYOA elements to place the reader in each of the existing *Star Wars* films and feature holograms on the covers.

2003 – With the series virtually out of print, the copyright licenses and the *Choose Your Own Adventure* trademark revert to R. A. Montgomery. He forms Chooseco LLC with Shannon Gilligan.

2005 – *Choose Your Own Adventure* is re-launched into the education market, with all new art and covers. Texts have been updated to reflect changes to technology and discoveries in archaeology and science.

2006 – Chooseco LLC, operating out of a renovated farmhouse in Waitsfield, Vermont, publishes the series for the North American retail market, shipping 900,000 copies in its first six months.

2008 – Chooseco publishes CYOA *The Golden Path*, a three volume epic for readers 10+, written by Anson Montgomery.

2008 – Poptropica and Chooseco partner to develop the first branded Poptropica island, "Nabooti Island" based on CYOA #4, *The Lost Jewels of Nabooti*.

2009 – *Choose Your Own Adventure* celebrates 30 years in print and releases two titles in partnership with WADA, the World Anti-Doping Agency, to emphasize fairness in sport.

2010 – Chooseco launches new look for the classic books using special neon ink in the famous CYOA frame..

2013 – Chooseco launches eBooks on Kindle and in the iBookstore with trackable maps and other bonus features. The project is briefly hung up when Apple has to rewrite its terms and conditions for publishers to create space for this innovative eBook type.

2014 – Brazil and Korea license publishing rights to the series. 20 foreign publishers currently distribute the series worldwide.

2014 – Beloved series founder R. A. Montgomery dies at age 78. He finishes his final book in the *Choose Your Own Adventure* series only weeks before.

2018 – Z-Man Games releases the first-ever Choose Your Own Adventure board game, adapted from *House of Danger*. Record sales lead to the creation of a new game for 2019 based on *War with the Evil Power Master*.

2019 – Chooseco publishes a new sub-series of Choose Your Own Adventure books based on real-life spies.

2019 – The first-ever *Choose Your Own Adventure* audiobooks are released, with voice-activated interactive technology.

2020 – Chooseco publishes baby books adapted from the first 3 CYOA classics and they are so popular a full reprint is ordered two months ahead of publication!

FORECAST FROM STONEHENGE

This book is different from other books.

You and YOU ALONE are in charge of what happens in this story.

There are dangers, choices, adventures, and consequences. YOU must use all of your numerous talents and much of your enormous intelligence. The wrong decision could end in disaster—even death. But don't despair. At any time, YOU can go back and make another choice, alter the path of your story, and change its result.

You travel to Stonehenge on the summer solstice, the most sacred day in the Druid calendar. You are supposed to meet a man named Alastair who knows something about the famously missing heelstone of Stonehenge. But when you arrive, the site is crowded with all sorts of people dressed in costume for the special day. You must exercise caution as not everyone is who they appear to be. If you find Alastair, he could lead you to archaeological fame and fortune—or to certain death. Are you ready to learn the ancient, dark secrets that Stonehenge has in store for you?

VISIT US ONLINE AT CYOA.COM